LOST
KING

flash
backs

This edition published 2014 by
A & C Black, an imprint of Bloomsbury Publishing Plc
50 Bedford Square, London, WC1B 3DP
www.bloomsbury.com
Bloomsbury is a registered trademark of Bloomsbury Publishing Plc

ISBN 978-1-4729-0440-9

A CIP catalogue for this book is available from the British Library.

Printed and bound by CPI Group (UK) Ltd, Croydon CR0 4YY

3 5 7 9 10 8 6 4 2

The
LOST
KING

Richard III and the
Princes in the Tower

ALISON PRINCE

A & C BLACK
AN IMPRINT OF BLOOMSBURY
LONDON NEW DELHI NEW YORK SYDNEY

Contents

Looking back

It's a long time ago now. My daughters and my son are almost grown up, and yet they still want to hear about what happened.

'You should write it down, Mama,' they say. 'You have told us, but nobody else knows, just you and Papa. And there are so many lies.'

A lot of people do know, more than my children suspect, but they dare not speak because the lies are powerful ones, designed to last forever.

Telling the truth may be the one thing I can do for my lost, beautiful boys and for the lost king who struggled so hard with the secrets and betrayals.

It seems like yesterday.

Perhaps that is the way to write it.

Just see it all over again, the way it was.

A strange beginning

March 1473

My father and I are driving out to see my granny in the next village. It's early spring, and primroses are blooming in the woods – a lovely day.

Papa is telling me about a woman who was digging turnips and put the fork clean through her foot when a horse comes galloping along the lane towards us.

The rider pulls it to a halt. 'Doctor Jones!' he gasps, 'There's been an accident at the Castle. The young prince had a fall. His uncle said please come at once.'

'Very well,' Papa says, calm as always. 'Lead the way and we'll follow.'

The rider turns his horse and sets off, looking over his shoulder. Papa urges our horse into a trot.

The gates of Ludlow Castle are standing open between its high, grey walls so we clatter straight into the courtyard. People are crowded round a fat woman who sits on the mounting block, holding a little boy in her lap. She's wearing an apron, so if he is the young prince, she can't be his mother. Queens do not wear aprons. Perhaps he *is* royal – there's a kind of dignity about him, though he's only small. His face is blotched with tears, but he's trying to push the woman's hand away as she dabs his swollen forehead with a cloth.

A man in elegant clothes comes towards us.

'Doctor Jones?'

'Yes,' says Papa.

'I am Earl Rivers, the boy's uncle. He was unconscious for several moments after a fall from his pony. He seems recovered, but as his guardian, I can take no chances.'

Papa hates time-wasters, but he says politely, 'You are wise, sir.'

He turns to the boy and says in his cheerful Welsh voice, 'Let's have a look, then.'

Papa holds the little boy's wrist for a moment, noting his pulse rate, then he puts a gentle finger under his chin to raise his head and inspects his eyes. He runs his hands through the fair, curling hair, feeling carefully for any damage to the skull, then turns to Earl Rivers.

'No cause for alarm as far as I can see,' he says, 'but it's quite a nasty graze. I'll put some salve on it. Make him more comfortable.'

Papa smoothes herbal ointment over the boy's forehead then covers the graze with a square of clean, soft linen from his leather bag. I often help him, so I know how to hold the cloth in place while he bandages the boy's head and ties the split ends in a neat bow.

'There you are, my handsome,' he says to his little patient. 'All tidy now.'

'Thank you,' the boy says. 'But you should call me Edward. Not what you said.'

'I beg your pardon, Edward,' Papa says gravely.

He glances at the coin Earl Rivers puts in his hand and says, 'This is too much, my lord. I have only been of simple service.'

'Maybe. But you have set my mind at rest, and that is of value. I am not experienced in the mishaps of children.'

Little Edward has begun to fidget. He's been sitting on the fat woman's lap for a long time, I expect, so he is getting bored. He needs something to play with. I run across to our horse and trap. I'd found a magpie's tail feather in the yard this morning and left it on the seat. I bring it back to him.

He scrambles down from the woman's lap and takes the feather. He runs its smooth length between his fingers and thumb then looks up, strangely excited about such a common thing.

'Is it for me?'

'Yes. A present.'

His face breaks into a beaming smile. 'Thank you!' he says.

He inspects the feather more carefully, as if it is something new to him. Perhaps he is more used to manufactured toys like rattles and puppets. Then he looks at me again and asks, 'What is your name?'

'Elizabeth,' I tell him, 'like your royal mother. But my brothers and sisters call me Lisa.'

'Lisa,' he repeats.

He stares at me again then runs to his uncle, who is still talking to Papa. He tugs at his coat, causing Earl Rivers to look down in surprise.

'What is it, Edward? You should not interrupt.'

'I want Lisa to stay here.'

People glance at each other but say nothing. After all, this child is a prince.

His uncle seems perplexed. 'Are you sure?'

'Yes,' the little boy says. 'I am sure. She is nice. I like her.'

Earl Rivers looks at me and asks, 'How old are you?'

'Twelve, sir.'

'She is the eldest of five,' Papa explains, 'so she is used to children.'

Edward takes my hand.

'I want her to stay,' he repeats. Then he adds, 'Please.'

It sounds like a word he seldom uses. He and I look at each other carefully. Neither of us smiles, but his hand tightens round mine.

Papa and Earl Rivers are talking together, so we have to wait and see if agreement comes. Edward holds the feather up to my face and I blow at it gently to make it flutter in his fingers. He laughs. I feel he does not laugh often.

Papa turns to me.

'Lisa,' he says. 'Earl Rivers would like you to be a companion and helper to this royal boy. But it means you will have to leave home and live here. The choice is yours. I cannot tell you what to do.'

Little Edward knows he must not pester, but his grey eyes are full of entreaty.

I'm scared and breathless, but in these few astonishing minutes, I have come to know that he needs me. How can this be? This child who will inherit a kingdom has everything, and I have nothing. But I cannot let him down. I start to answer but my voice doesn't seem to be working properly, so I take a shaky breath and try again.

'Yes,' I manage to say. 'I would like to.'

Earl Rivers tells Papa, 'Bring her back tomorrow with her things.'

Things? I have only a shawl and a spare dress, and a comb for my hair.

Edward is not absolutely sure his wish has been granted. He asks, 'You promise?'

'Yes,' I tell him. 'I promise.'

'Good,' he says.

Papa and I climb back into the trap. He slaps the reins gently on the horse's back and we move forward through the gateway to the road outside. I feel as if I'm dreaming.

'Well,' Papa says. 'Your granny will be surprised. And your mother, too. I hope we have done the right thing.'

My fingers are crossed. With a magpie's feather that cost nothing, it seems I have bought a new life.

So much to learn

May 1473

They said my clothes would not do, and gave me two blue dresses and black leather shoes. I wear a clean apron every day and my hair has to be tucked into a white cap. I still feel like a new, strange person, but I am getting used to it.

Edward is an easy child to amuse. He has no brothers or sisters here to play with, so he welcomes my company in his free time – not that he has much of that, poor little soul. He does not have to collect firewood and look for mushrooms and help weed the garden as we do in our family, but in many ways, his life is more severe. His uncle, whom people always call Rivers, expects him to work hard at his learning.

He has a tutor called Dr Alcock – not a medical doctor like Papa, though. He is the Bishop of Worcester, a stern man, though he is careful with his little pupil and never unkind.

Edward's Uncle Richard, the Duke of Gloucester, has been here several times. He is the King's youngest brother. He brings small gifts, but what Edward really likes is that he treats him as an intelligent fellow-person, not a mere child. They get on wonderfully well. Richard is married to Anne Neville, who is slim like him, with a bright, smiling face. They have a young baby, a little boy called Edward, like his cousin. Royal people seem to use the same names all the time.

Richard is not much taller than I am, though they say his brother, the King, is a giant of a man. Richard has a thin, kind face, with grey eyes like his little nephew's and dark eyebrows. There is a wary look to him sometimes, like a dog that lifts its head at a sound nobody else has heard. Had he really been a dog, people might have called him the runt of the litter, for his back is not quite straight and one shoulder is a little higher than the other. I've heard him sneered at as 'Richard Crookback', but that is unkind, because he is strong and wiry. And he carries his cloak tossed over that shoulder, so you hardly see any lack of straightness. Papa thinks swaddling babies tightly when they are born, as so many people do, can cause a curvature of the spine. My brothers and sisters were free to kick their little legs – but I can see it saves a lot of bother if babies are made into tight little parcels that can be hung on any handy peg.

Papa told me a lot about Richard. He was only eight years old when his father and eldest brother were killed in a battle. After that, he lived in the house of a man called Richard Neville, Earl of Warwick, who was his guardian, just as Rivers is guardian to Edward. Richard's wife, Anne, is Warwick's daughter. They met as children, and loved each other even then. But Papa says Warwick turned out to be a treacherous enemy to Richard. No wonder he is watchful.

Little Edward will not see his uncle so often from now on, because the King has made Richard the governor of the North of England. Annie, the fat woman who was sitting with Edward on her lap when I first saw him, is the cook here, and she knows everything. She says the North is a wild, hilly place rather like Wales, but colder.

Edward made no fuss when his Uncle Richard told him he had to go away, just pressed his lips together

17

and nodded. He was given the title of Prince of Wales when he was just a baby, and tries hard to be grown up. When he is old enough, he will govern Wales and the Marches surrounding Ludlow Castle. And of course, he will be the King of England when his father dies. So he is serious about everything, and works hard at his lessons.

Our days follow a strict pattern. We rise early, while it is still dark. I sleep in the same room as Edward, in case he should wake at night. I help him wash and dress, then we go to Matins and hear Mass. We have breakfast then he studies with his tutor. He already reads very well. Dr Alcock has a huge, heavy Bible, in a language I don't understand. Edward says it is from Germany. It is not made by hand, but printed by a wonderful machine.

Earl Rivers is stern about the way the servants behave. He is very strict about how we speak, for the King has said his son must not at any time hear swear words or 'ribald language'. Annie laughed when she heard that and said, 'Better keep my mouth shut, then, hadn't I?'

Annie has worked in this castle since she was a girl, and her mother before her. She is the chief cook now and a great gossip, but wonderfully kind. She has told me a lot about the royal people we serve, though I don't see much of them, as my days and nights are fully taken up with Edward.

When his morning lessons end at about ten o'clock, we have dinner, then I take him upstairs for a short rest. Rivers wanted to know the reason, but I didn't have a reason, I was just doing what Mama always did. I told him my father says children need time after a meal to digest their food. He accepted that, so the first lesson after dinner starts a little later now.

The afternoon is for what the outdoor tutors call 'sport'. I call it play, though it is only play when I am allowed to join in. We run and jump and dance and sing songs, but that never goes on for very long, because there are more serious aims. Edward is instructed in the proper way to throw a ball or a stone to hit a target, and he learns the formal moves of fencing, using a straight stick because he is too young for a sword. Yesterday, one of the huntsmen showed him how to fit an arrow to the small-sized bow that has been made for him. He found it hard to take the strain of the string, but the man was stern.

'You must hold the bow steady, young sir,' he said, 'so you can release the arrow cleanly.'

Edward went on trying, though his little arms were trembling. Sometimes I could weep for him, the way he works so hard.

We have supper at about four, after evensong. At eight the candles are lit and the curtains are drawn for bedtime. When I first came here, Rivers was surprised that I could read and seemed pleased. He gave me a list of instructions about preparations for the night. The boy must be 'merry and joyous', it says, in the time before going to bed, so that he sleeps peacefully, with happy dreams. And that is right, of course. After a prayer, I tuck him into bed and tell him a story, then stay with him until his eyes are closed. I myself sleep as lightly as a cat, ready to wake at any sound, but little Edward sleeps deep and peacefully.

***

I help Annie in the kitchen while Edward is at his lessons. She is constantly busy, plucking fowls and butchering meat and making bread and cakes, but she keeps up a stream of conversation. Tom Owen, the youngest of the gardeners, said, 'Nice to have someone new to all the gossip, eh, Annie?' Then ducked to avoid the mock cuff she aimed at him.

Annie is whipping cream for a trifle now, and I'm on the other side of the table, chopping a pile of parsnips. There's something I want to ask her.

'Ever since I was small, there have been battles, but I don't really know what they're about. Do you?'

'York and Lancaster, you silly girl. The Lancaster family ruled until our King Edward was crowned. Edward is of York, of course.'

'Papa says the Lancaster king went mad.'

'Yes. King Henry the Sixth. He was never much good at ruling. Should have been a monk really – always praying and singing hymns. But he got worse. Babbled like a baby, they say, didn't understand anything. His wife was running the country, but that couldn't go on.'

'So they asked our King Edward to take over?'

Annie rolls her eyes.

'For goodness' sake! Edward belongs to the *York* family, so he was the Lancastrians' enemy.'

'Oh, I see. So they fought for the crown? And Edward won?'

'After a lot of ups and downs, yes. It ended with a huge battle at Towton. They fought all day in a blizzard. Twenty-eight thousand men were killed. Twenty-eight *thousand* – can you imagine? While that was happening, Warwick and his men took over London. He gave it to Edward like a pig's head on a plate. "Here you are, boy – a present."'

'Who is Warwick?'

'Richard Neville, Earl of Warwick. Just about the most powerful man in England. And a treacherous piece of work if ever there was one. He was guardian to King Edward as a young boy, same as Earl Rivers is guardian to little Edward now. But Warwick deserted him when the Lancasters took power, and went with them instead – until old King Henry lost his wits. Warwick thought our Edward would probably become king then, so he switched back again and fought on Edward's side at Towton.'

'Thank goodness for that.'

'It wasn't Warwick's last change, though. One Christmas morning, the mad old king came downstairs, perfectly sane. Or so they said.'

'Wasn't it true, then?'

'Put it this way – the Lancasters needed it to be true. Their army had been wiped out. Warwick had left them. Henry had a baby son but he was too small to be any use. King Henry was their only hope, and a slender one, at that. Edward of York had everything going for him. But then he made his terrible mistake.'

Annie puts her bowl of cream, thick now, on a marble slab. She drops the whisk into the sink then sits down again.

'What mistake?'

'He married Elizabeth Woodville.'

I'm startled. 'Our Queen?'

'Our Queen,' Annie agrees grimly. 'What a disaster. Warwick was furious. He had a French princess lined up to be Edward's wife. Stronger ties between two royal families, more power for both of them.'

'And for Warwick.'

'Exactly. But Edward was only twenty-two. That may sound old to you, Lisa, but men are not much more than boys at that age, and being king had gone to his head. You can see it, can't you? Everyone bowing and scraping and girls falling into bed with him at the lift of an eyebrow. He thought one more common trollop would be no different from the rest.'

'*Elizabeth?* A common – '

'Ssh!' Annie hisses. 'Keep your voice down. All right, her family is aristocratic. But the Woodvilles are not royal.'

'So why did Edward – '

'*Marry* her? Funny, isn't it? He never married any of his other mistresses, not even Jane Shore, though

23

he still adores her. But you see,' Annie goes on, 'Elizabeth's first husband, Sir John Grey, had been killed in battle and left her with two sons. She wasn't going to be any man's mistress – she wanted a new husband. And she was aiming at the top.'

'How did she meet the King?'

'Stood in front of him with her two young boys when he was out riding. Begged him to restore her dead husband's estate. He'd fought for Lancaster, of course, so his lands were confiscated when the York side won. Edward took one look at her and wanted her like mad. She knew it, of course – that was what she'd been hoping for. Wherever he went after that, there she was, looking beautiful and seductive. You know how she is.'

'Well – yes.'

I blush a little to think of it. Elizabeth and the King were here not long ago, and he could hardly keep his hands off her, though she is hugely pregnant just now. But she is fabulously beautiful, with that blonde hair and sleepy, inviting eyes. At the evening meal, they were so taken up with their exchanged glances and laughter and touching of hands that food hardly mattered. They'd barely have finished their main course before Edward would push his chair back and lead her up to their bedchamber, dessert left untouched on the table.

'Elizabeth was more than willing to exchange kisses and caresses,' Annie goes on, 'but any more than that, she went all prim. Said the joys of her body were only for the man who would marry her. It drove Edward mad. He wasn't used to being thwarted.'

'So he gave in.'

'Yes.' Annie looks thoughtful. 'Maybe she promised to go on being his little secret – who knows? But the minute the ring was on her finger, she demanded her rights as the Queen of England. Next thing, Ludlow Castle is full of her relatives, all of them with peerages and high office. As you may have noticed.'

'Like Earl Rivers?'

'He was the first, but there are dozens more. Everyone in this court is either a Woodville or a Woodville supporter. Even Dr Alcock, though he tries to keep it quiet.'

'What about Uncle Richard?'

'He loathed the Woodvilles. Still does. But he had to keep the peace for Edward's sake. If you ask me,' Annie adds, 'he'll be glad to get away to Yorkshire, out of it all. People up there love him. They say he is a fair ruler – listens to complaints and requests. Clarence is still here, though, stirring up trouble.'

'Who is he?'

'Richard's elder brother. George, Duke of Clarence. He's so furious about Edward's stupid marriage, he's been conspiring against him with Warwick ever since.'

'Warwick? You mean, he changed sides *again*?'

'Yes. The marriage with Elizabeth wrecked his plans, so he rejoined the Lancastrians. And spread rumours that King Edward had no right to rule because he was illegitimate. Said he was the bastard son of an archer called Blaybourne.'

'Annie!' I'm shocked. 'Is that true?'

'Heaven knows. But anyway, Warwick and Clarence led a Lancaster army against Edward, and won. They took Edward prisoner. Warwick suggested he himself should wear the crown, in Edward's place. But the public wouldn't have that. They threatened rebellion, so Parliament released Edward and said he must go on ruling.'

'Did Edward imprison Clarence and Warwick?' I ask.

'No,' Annie says. 'You won't believe this, but he offered them friendship. Said they should write the whole thing off as a misunderstanding and work together in the future.'

'After they'd tried to kill him? But why?'

'Strange, isn't it.' Annie eyes me carefully, as if wondering how much to tell. When she goes on, I don't know what she's decided. 'Clarence and Warwick were still working for Lancaster. They went to Margaret of Anjou, old King Henry's wife, who was back in France, and asked her to give them an army, so they could help restore her husband to the throne.'

'And did she?'

'Oh, yes. She never gave up fighting for what she saw as her rights. There was a tremendous battle. But Edward and Richard won.'

'Uncle Richard? Did he fight as well?'

'Yes. He was only seventeen – his first battle. There were more. At the last one, Warwick was killed. Clarence knew he was beaten, so he came to Edward and apologised.'

'Was that the end of it?'

Annie sighs. 'Will we ever see an end? But at the time, it was the end of the Lancasters. King Henry and Margaret of Anjou's son died in that same battle and he'd been heir to the throne. He was married to Warwick's daughter, Anne Neville.'

'But she's Uncle Richard's wife! Was she married before, then?'

'Yes, but not by her choice. She and Richard had loved each other since they were children, but her father betrothed her to mad Henry's son – the future king. A far better catch than Richard Crookback, youngest of four brothers.'

'But after the battle, Anne was free again,' I say, wanting some good news in all this. 'A happy ending.'

'Not yet. Clarence knew Anne had inherited masses of land and wealth, so he said he was the elder brother and Anne must marry him, not Richard. Oh, what a quarrel there was! It went on for weeks. Richard was desperate to marry Anne. But Clarence tried to steal her by force. She escaped from his house disguised as a servant girl.'

'Heavens!'

'Edward had to give a judgement, as the King. He ruled that Anne would be Richard's wife and Clarence could marry her older sister, Isabel – with a share of the wealth and estates.'

'So everyone was happy.'

'Not quite. Margaret of Anjou had lost her son, her only child. And her husband – '

Annie's face clouds.

'Her husband?' I prompt. 'Mad old Henry?'

'It was terrible, Lisa. Henry had been in the battle, though I doubt if he knew what was going on, poor man. Edward took him prisoner, and there was a great banquet in the Tower of London to celebrate the victory. Later on, when the King and Queen had gone to bed, we heard Elizabeth shouting in their room. Edward had said he was going out, and she was furious. She wanted to know what could matter to him more than his wife, after so long away. But he wouldn't tell her. He just said there was something he had to do.'

'What was it?'

'Next morning, the guards found old King Henry dead in his prison cell.'

'You can't mean – ' I'm aghast. 'Edward wouldn't do that. It must have been someone else.'

'Henry was in the *Tower*, Lisa. Portcullis at the drawbridge, cannon all round the battlements, armed soldiers everywhere. Who else could have walked in there, unchallenged?'

Annie takes a breath.

'Who else could have had the key?'

I feel cold to my bones.

A brother for Edward

17th August 1473

The Queen has had her new baby – and it is a boy, a little brother for Edward! Everyone was hoping for a boy, so there are great celebrations. Edward has two elder sisters, and the baby born last year was a girl as well, but she died within a few days, poor little thing. This baby prince is strong and healthy, and his name will be Richard of Shrewsbury.

***

Tom Owen was in the hayloft this morning, eating an apple and sheltering from the rain, when he heard

Clarence come into the stable below him with another man. Tom kept as still as a mouse, and heard every word they said. They were planning a new attack on the King. I said Tom should tell Earl Rivers, but I know he will not. Some things are too dangerous to meddle in.

Tom is like my father in many ways. Though he is not a doctor, he is skilled and careful, with strong hands that can haul a tree root from the ground or nurse a tender seedling. I like his curly brown hair and dark eyes and his straight white teeth. He likes me, too, but I must not fall in love with him. When Edward's new brother comes here, there will be more to do, not less – and royal children do not find much love and laughter except with the servants who care for them.

**

It is 1475 now. And I have been to London! For a few days, young Edward had to be his father's deputy while the King went to France. It seemed there was going to be a war, but they signed a treaty, thank goodness, so we are back at Ludlow now.

It was a lot to ask of a young child. Edward tried his best to be grown up, but he often looked strained and worried. The Queen was running everything, but whatever she did had to be agreed by Edward on the King's behalf. A pantomime, but a serious one.

Edward will go on living at Ludlow until he is fourteen. I am glad of that, and hope they will not call on him too often to perform these state duties. It is good to be back here. I never thought this castle would feel like home, but compared with the crowded, dirty city, it is tranquil and familiar, if not exactly welcoming.

June 1477

The Duke of Clarence, Uncle Richard's older brother, has been arrested. Tom never told anyone about the conversation he overheard, but the King found out somehow. Although Clarence has been so treacherous, I can't help feeling sorry for him. His wife, Isabel, died three days before Christmas after giving birth to a baby son and a few days later the baby died as well. The two older children are going to live with Uncle Richard and his wife, Anne. She is their aunt, and she only has the one son. People say she is not well, but I expect their servants will take good care of the children.

9th November 1477

We have been to London again. It was Edward's seventh birthday last week, so there was a state banquet to celebrate it. He had to play the host. He did it beautifully, dressed in silk and velvet, with a coronet on his curly head. The King and Queen were there, and countless notabilities, including Uncle Richard and Anne with their own son and Clarence's son and daughter. Rivers was there, and Dr Alcock, and Elizabeth Woodville's grown-up sons from her first marriage, and countless other Woodville relatives.

Rivers has translated a book from French into English. It is called *The Dictes and Sayings of the Philosophers*. William Caxton, who was at the banquet as well, is going to print it. Caxton has been abroad in Bruges, learning about wonderful new machines that that can make copies of a book in great numbers. He came home to set up a printing press of his own, and the book translated by Rivers will be the first ever to be printed in England. So that was another cause for celebration.

15th January 1478

We have been to London yet again. This time I saw more of Edward's little brother, Richard. He has the same fair, curling hair and angelic face as Edward. It is planned that he will come to join us at Ludlow later this month, for he is almost the same age as Edward was when I first saw him. Far too young, I thought, for the ceremony we had to attend. At barely four years old, he was being married to Anne Mowbray, daughter of the Duke of Norfolk. She is just six, a slender little girl with a pale, serious face and a mass of red hair escaping from a coronet that looked too big and heavy for her.

These royal children are like puppies traded between dog breeders for their future potential. I don't like to see them pushed into such use when they are hardly more than babies, but that is how the strange world of these privileged people works.

***

Little Prince Richard is with us now. He is a gentle boy, less serious than his older brother, perhaps because he is not burdened by knowing he will one day be the king. I am doing my best to ensure that we settle down together comfortably as three instead of two. I take care that Edward shall have no cause for jealousy, or that Richard shall feel left out, and they seem to get on very well together. Edward enjoys his superiority, knowing the Castle and everyone in it, but he is very sweet to his little brother.

Neither of the boys has the solid build of their massive father. With their slim build and fair hair inherited from Elizabeth, they look like those paintings of angels on cathedral walls. When I see their two golden heads together, talking or engrossed by something they are playing with, it fills me with delight.

Edward is taking great pride in helping his younger brother to improve his reading – and it is not difficult, for Richard is a clever child and learns very quickly. They have occasional arguments, but they are great friends. For me, it is fascinating to watch them grow and learn. The days spent with them are a constant joy and they are going to be such fine young men.

Trouble brewing

February 1478

The King and Queen are here, visiting their sons. I should not say this, but I wish they had not come. Wherever she goes, Elizabeth Woodville brings constant demands and unrest. This morning's episode was typical. We heard her shouting at Edward in their royal bedchamber, which is close enough to our room for the boys to hear every word.

'George is a traitor, Edward. You know he is. Everyone knows. How much longer are you going to wait?'

The King said coldly, 'The Duke of Clarence is no concern of yours.'

But she ranted on.

'He is *everyone's* concern. It is outrageous that – '

I began to talk loudly about something trivial, trying to drown her words, but Edward held up his hand to hush me. He is nearly nine now, and has a natural authority that cannot be ignored. So I fell silent, and Elizabeth's furious voice was terribly clear.

'Your brother has been guilty of treason a hundred times over. If he were a common man you'd have sent him to the block years ago and thought nothing of it. Why should he be favoured and escape execution? People are saying you have lost your courage.'

'That is not true. You know perfectly well – '

But she cut through his words.

'Are you admitting that you love your treacherous brother more than you love justice?'

The King's voice was quiet and angry. 'Elizabeth. You know the reason.'

'That old tale? Pah! Of course I know – who better? Why are you worried? We can deal with any troublemakers – you have the power. But you must *use* your power, Edward. I am sick of your cowardice and dithering. Whose side are you on – George's or mine? Make up your mind, before he makes it up for you.'

The door slammed, and we heard the clacking of her high-heeled shoes as she ran down the stairs.

Richard's face was white and his lips were trembling. I tried to take him on my lap, but he pulled away. Edward had more sense. He spoke to his little brother cheerfully.

'Grown-ups have arguments sometimes. Don't worry about it.'

He reached for a knitted stocking and slipped his hand into it, then wriggled it towards Richard.

'A big snake coming to get you,' he said. 'Sssssssssssss!'

Richard began to fend the woolly snake off and laughed, unwillingly at first.

Edward looked at me over the top of his head as he went on gently buffeting his brother.

'My mother is right, Lisa,' he said. 'The King has to show his hand.'

He never calls his father Papa, just *the King*. I did not know what to say. All I know is, I am full of fear.

***

The boys are outside, doing their sporting activities. I am in the kitchen, helping Annie to pluck chickens and telling her about the Queen's tirade this morning – but the door bursts open and men from the royal guard come clattering in. They are red-faced and excited, laughing yet somehow shocked.

Annie's brother is one of them. She asks, 'Jack, what's happened?'

'The King's brother,' he says. 'The Duke of Clarence. Arrested, tried, condemned to death. We've just escorted him back to the Tower.'

'He's been asking for it for years,' Annie says. 'Sit down, you lot, you're making the place untidy.'

She goes over to the barrel of ale in the corner and starts filling mugs.

'Lisa, hand these out.'

The men are unbuckling belts, undoing tunics, dumping their swords and scabbards on the floor, pulling out chairs, sitting down. Laughing, clinking mugs together, shoving the chickens out of the way so feathers fly around. It's going to be a party.

'What are they going to do with him?' Annie asks after a bit. 'They can't hang the King's brother like some common criminal.'

'Special treat,' Jack says, grinning. 'Big privilege. They've said he can choose how he wants to die. Got to make up his mind by tomorrow morning. Cheers. Here's to justice.'

'Here's to justice!' they chorus, clinking mugs again. Ale slops over. The serious drinking begins.

***

We know now how Clarence chose to die, although Annie reckons it was someone else's choice, not his. They found his body in a huge barrel of red wine. So Annie is probably right. He was helped, as she put it.

There are a lot of people in the kitchen again, not soldiers, just the servants who work here. This is our natural meeting place when something has happened.

'Clarence always liked a drink,' a man says, and everyone laughs.

Annie says, 'I hope they don't chuck it away just because he's been in it. Malmsey's a lovely marinade for venison.'

I find it hard to join in the merriment. Perhaps because my father has compassion for those who die, I'm appalled by what has happened. The luxurious life of this castle has shown a nasty underside, like turning over a dead bird and finding it full of maggots. For the first time in all these years, I almost wish I had gone home with my father and stayed there, that day when Edward fell from his pony.

Too late now. Conflict and betrayal and killing are part of the way these privileged people live. As well as caring for the boys and keeping them happy, I may need to protect them, though I do not know from what or whom.

21ˢᵗ November 1481

Anne Mowbray, the little girl who was married with such ceremony to Richard two years ago, died last week. So the dog-breeders will have to pick a new bride to mate with their pedigree prince. I think of her white, serious face and wild red hair, and grieve for her. Increasingly often these days, I wish I could take my lovely boys away from this mad place and let them grow up as I did, in a simple house where we worked hard and did nothing to harm anyone.

Shock

14th April 1483

I cannot believe it.

King Edward died five days ago. The messenger who came would not speak to any of us until he had given the letter to Earl Rivers, who came when summoned, looking a little irritable at the interruption to his writing.

He read the letter, and his expression changed. He closed his eyes and took a deep breath, then made the sign of the cross. All of us did likewise, though we did not know what he was going to tell us.

His voice was quiet and dry.

'The King is dead.'

In the gasps and moans that followed, he looked at the letter again, as if hardly believing it. Then he turned to me and said, 'Tell Edward to come to my room at once. Do not mention the reason.'

Edward was alone with Dr Alcock, as Richard is in London with his mother. He took one look at my face and got to his feet.

'Lisa, what is it?'

'Your uncle asks you to go to him.'

'Now? At once?'

'Yes.'

We walked up the stairs in silence, though there was so much I wanted to say. Edward stopped and turned to me, frowning.

'Something has happened, hasn't it?'

I nodded. There was an ache in my throat and I longed to give him what comfort I could, but orders had to be obeyed.

'Earl Rivers has to tell you,' I said.

I think he knew then. He said nothing, but for the first time since he was small, he took my hand. He is twelve now, and taller than I am. When we reached his uncle's room, he tapped on the door.

'Come in,' Rivers said.

Since then, we have been in turmoil. Messengers keep arriving from London. They dismount from sweating horses and run up the stairs with letters for Rivers.

Uncle Richard was with King Edward when he died. He is the only one left of the royal brothers now, and Edward appointed him to be the official protector of his young nephews. I am glad of that.

It seems sad that a great king who survived countless battles should die of what started as a common cold – though I must admit, Edward had grown fat and red-faced in the last year or two, and drank far too much. The servants often had to carry him to bed because he was too drunk to stand or walk.

Young Edward is now Edward the Fifth, King of England. He is going to London for his coronation very soon, with an armed guard. I am to go as well, to take care of Edward's possessions and make sure he has whatever he needs.

My father rode here after he heard the news. He seemed worried. 'Lisa, this visit to London may last a long time,' he said. 'Edward may never come back to Ludlow. What is to happen to you?'

'I don't know. But I have to go.'

'Yes. I can see that. Look – keep this carefully.' He gave me a name and address written on a piece of paper. 'This is your Uncle Bryn, my younger brother. You were still a baby the one time he came to see us, so you won't remember him. He is a cabinet-maker, makes fine furniture for the gentry. His wife's name is Olwen. They live in Fleet Lane, near the river. I've sent them a letter. It should be there by now – the postal service Richard set up is a blessing. Promise me you'll visit them, Lisa. I want to be sure you have somewhere to go if you need help.'

The idea that I may need help makes me newly afraid. Ludlow Castle is a world of its own, but it has become my home. Maybe we will take some of that world to London. I wish Annie could come, but she has to stay here.

***

Tom and I have come to the forest glade we think of as our own. We stand with our arms round each other. My face is buried in the warmth of his jacket.

He says, 'I wish you weren't going to London.'

'So do I.'

And it is true. I love Tom, though I tried hard not to. I want so much to stay with him – but I cannot desert the boys. Their Uncle Richard's motto is 'Loyauté Me Lie', which Dr Alcock said means 'Loyalty Binds Me'. I, too, feel bound.

'Things are so uncertain. And the boys are still young. It would be an unkind time to leave them.'

'Lisa, their world is not our world,' Tom says. 'Their wars and deaths and riches are nothing to do with us. I want you to marry me. Let the boys go. Please. We can have children of our own.'

I feel torn in half.

'I love you, Tom, I really do. I want to marry you. But can we wait just a little longer?'

'Anyone who waits for things to be safe and certain is a fool,' he says. 'And I hope I am not a fool.' He sighs. 'But yes, I will wait for you.'

'Oh, Tom! Thank you, thank you. It won't be long, I promise. I'll come back as soon as I can.'

We kiss again. I wish we could stay here longer, but the sun is low in the sky behind the trees.

Packing up

Annie sits down on the box we have just tied with rope, hands in her lap.

'The wolves are out, Lisa,' she says.

'Wolves?'

'Enemies.'

'But – things are all right now, aren't they? The Lancaster side is beaten. It doesn't have an heir to the throne.'

'Oh, yes, it does,' Annie says grimly. 'They've found themselves a new one. Henry Tudor. He's lived in France most of his life. Claims to be descended from the ancient Welsh king, Cadwalladr, which means nothing at all. Any Welsh person could say the same.'

'Isn't he royal, then?'

'Only through a bastard line. His grand-da was a page in the court of Henry the Fifth. He seduced the king's widow, who bore him a son called Edmund Tudor. That Edmund was this Henry Tudor's father.'

'So why do they think he should be king?'

'You may well ask. The thing is, Henry Tudor's mother is now married to Lord Stanley, and he's as two-faced as Warwick was. Everyone says he's going to help Henry Tudor to invade England and take the throne by force.'

I'm horrified.

'But he can't! Young Edward is the king!'

Annie frowns down at her hands, and makes no answer. I'm suddenly afraid.

'Annie, what is it?'

She sighs.

'I've never told you this, Lisa. There's an old secret – but it won't stay secret much longer, the way things are going. The King's marriage to Elizabeth Woodville wasn't his first one.'

That's an old tale, so I'm relieved.

'Yes, he was engaged to someone else, they say. But isn't it just gossip?'

'No. It's true. And it wasn't just an engagement. Edward married Lady Eleanor Butler, months before Elizabeth grabbed him.'

'Actually *married* her?'

'Yes. And the wolves are hunting around to prove it. They want it known that the King's marriage to Elizabeth broke the law. I know this is hard, Lisa, but – Edward's children are not legal. Your lovely boys have no more claim to the throne than their illegitimate brothers and sisters that nobody knows about.'

My hands are over my mouth in a long gasp of horror. 'Annie! No!'

'I'm sorry. I know what they mean to you.'

'How long have you known?'

'I've always known. Some things are best not talked about.'

Coming from Annie, that would be laughable, were it not so frightening.

'Does Uncle Richard know?'

'Of course he does.'

No wonder he looks wary.

Annie goes on, 'Richard is the youngest brother, so he never dreamed of being king. But Clarence, the middle one, was second to Edward, and he more than dreamed of it, he thought he had a right. He was furious about the marriage to Elizabeth, and even more furious about being forced to keep the secret, to protect the York family from scandal and downfall.'

'Yes, of course.'

'Clarence had no guilty marriage hidden away, so he felt he should rule,' Annie goes on. 'And of course Warwick was spreading this rumour that his brother, King Edward, was himself illegitimate. Nonsense, if you ask me – a typical bit of Warwick mischief. But it gave Clarence even more reason to want his older brother out of the way.'

'*That's* why he and Warwick kept conspiring!'

'Yes. And that's partly what the wars were about. If Edward could be killed in battle, it would be nobody's fault. Clarence would be crowned king and the York family name – and his mother's reputation – wouldn't be dragged in the mud. Without Edward, Elizabeth would lose her power to get favours for the Woodvilles, so they would cause no trouble. But Edward was such a good fighter, they simply couldn't kill him.'

'So Clarence went on keeping the secret.'

'He had to. Elizabeth controlled everyone. Edward gave her whatever she demanded, because she could destroy him whenever she chose. All she had to do was act the innocent and say she'd just found out about a previous wife, and he'd be finished. And, of course, he was still completely infatuated with her, so he didn't mind.'

Trying to be fair, I say, 'Perhaps she really didn't know about the earlier marriage.'

Annie snorts with contempt.

'Of course she did! Elizabeth's mother was Jacquetta of Luxembourg. She knew everyone and everything – people said she was a witch, they were quite scared of her. Jacquetta saw from the start that her daughter could blackmail the King if she could make him marry her. And she was right.'

A thought comes to my grieving mind. 'The morning when the boys and I heard the Queen shouting at Edward, she said "that old tale" shouldn't worry him.'

'What she meant was, keeping it secret didn't worry Clarence,' Annie says. 'Not any more. Think of it, Lisa. He was imprisoned in the Tower and knew he'd be executed sooner or later. His wife was dead. Warwick, too.'

'He had nothing to lose.'

'Exactly. So why not tell everyone the secret? At least they'd know he'd had a justifiable claim to be King when Edward died. Elizabeth was desperately afraid he would talk. Edward was afraid as well, once she made him face it. Think how fast he acted, that morning when you heard her shouting at him. Clarence was tried, condemned and back in the Tower before he could say a word to anyone. Dead a few hours later.'

I can see it all, and I'm frightened.

'What will she do now?'

'Elizabeth?' Annie shrugs. 'The Lord knows. With Edward gone, she'll get no more support from the house of York. They hate her, and always have – with good reason. The talk is that she's toadying up to the Lancasters, and I think that's true. She's offered them her eldest daughter as a wife for Henry Tudor.'

'I know. But – surely she wants to see Edward on the throne? He's her son.'

But another awful truth dawns and I smack a hand to my head.

'No! She knows he can't rule. She's known all along. It could have worked if the secret had held, but

Edward is no use to her now. Neither is his brother. They never will be.' I feel sick with horror.

We stare at each other.

Annie asks, 'Do you think young Edward knows the secret, Lisa? You've been closer to him than most.'

I shake my head.

'I'm sure he doesn't.'

Ever since he was small, Edward has shown no doubt about his future kingship. I can see now, they had to make sure he believed it. Little boys can betray secrets without meaning to. Perhaps that is why he was sent to Rivers at such an early age, to be kept in careful seclusion where he could hear no rumours. The only people he saw at Ludlow either knew nothing, like the archers and sportsmen, or could be relied on, like Dr Alcock and Uncle – heavens! I gasp as it hits me.

'Uncle Richard! He's the last royal brother. If the boys can't inherit the throne, *he* must be the king.'

Annie looks at me wearily.

'Have you only just seen that? Silly girl – of *course* he must. But Richard is Elizabeth's worst enemy. She'll do anything to keep him from being crowned.'

'They will try to kill him,' I say with cold certainty.

'Yes. Richard knows that. He'll make sure he is well guarded. But this won't get the packing done.'

Annie gets to her feet and pushes her sleeves up then gives me a stern stare.

'And listen, young Lisa – you will not repeat a word of this conversation to anyone.'

'Of course not.'

I'd be too terrified.

21ˢᵗ April 1483

We started on the long journey to London this morning. Horses, riders, baggage carts – and masses of heavily armed soldiers. People say there are two thousand of them. Two *thousand*! They have carts piled with guns, some of them so heavy that they need teams of four horses. Looking back and forward along the procession, I cannot see its end or beginning. It is as though we are marching to war.

All the important people from the castle are with us, Earl Rivers, Dr Alcock, John Vaughan who is the castle treasurer, Elizabeth Woodville's two sons from her first marriage. The older one, Thomas, is entrusted with much of the castle's management. Elizabeth herself is in sanctuary with young Richard and her daughters, in Westminster. Uncle Richard is to meet us at a place called Northampton.

30th April 1483

We did not stop at Northampton, though we'd been looking forward to unsaddling the horses and getting something to eat. Rivers apologised for the extra hours of riding. He said the Queen had ordered the change. As Elizabeth is in London, I think this cannot be true. It must have been planned. Anyway, we continued on to this place called Stony Stratford and settled into various inns for the night. Then Rivers and Thomas Grey took fresh horses and rode back to Northampton to wait for Richard.

They came back this morning. Richard was with them, and so was Henry Stafford, the Duke of Buckingham, who had come from London to meet them in Northampton, with a troop of three hundred men.

Buckingham is married to Elizabeth Woodville's sister, Catherine. It was he who signed George's death warrant. He is a thick-lipped, narrow-eyed man. Annie said she would not trust him with a pet rat. But he is on Richard's side – at least, for now. He told him that Rivers, Grey and Vaughan were hatching a massive plot against him.

Buckingham's servants told us what happened last night. There was a grand dinner in Northampton, as you would expect. Wine was drunk and everyone had a good time. Afterwards, Buckingham and Richard talked together for most of the night. At dawn, Buckingham's men arrested Rivers and the other two.

I still can't believe it. They got Rivers out of a cart with his hands tied, hustled him into an upstairs room and locked the door. Vaughan and Grey as well. They will be taken to Pontefract Castle in Yorkshire, to stand trial. People say they will be executed.

There must be some reason why Rivers brought us to Stony Stratford then rode all the way back to Northampton. I think it can only be because he did not want Richard to see the carts laden with guns and armaments. We know now that Rivers, Grey and Vaughan were secretly on Henry Tudor's side, together with the rest of the Woodvilles. The weapons were intended to arm a fleet of ships they planned to build, so they could guard Henry's fleet when he came from France to invade England. It was high treason.

Poor young Edward was outraged to see Rivers, in whose house he has lived since he was small, stumbling in with his hands tied. Uncle Richard took him aside and spoke to him quietly for quite a long time. Edward listened and stopped protesting, but afterwards his face was white and troubled. Richard is going to take him the rest of the way to London, and I am glad of that. I have to go on with the rest of the procession, but most of the servants are going back to Ludlow. I think of Tom, and wish I could be with them. But there may still be things I can do for Edward.

London

4th May 1483

When we reached the great city, Uncle Richard took Edward to the Bishop's Palace in St Paul's Churchyard. With some other servants, I waited outside the closed door of the room where they were, to see if we would be needed.

Edward came out with his uncle and the Bishop and some other men. He looked tired, and older than his twelve years. He saw me, and I curtsied to him. He raised me to my feet and said quietly, 'I have much to thank you for, Lisa. But I am a man now. I will not need you while we are here. When things have settled down, we will meet again.'

He kissed me on the forehead.

I will always remember that.

5th May 1483

Richard's wife, Anne Neville, is here now, with Clarence's orphaned children and their own little boy. I am helping to look after them, perhaps needlessly, as Anne has plenty of servants. But it is better to have something to do, as I have seen no more of Edward and feel useless.

Richard is organising everything for the coronation on 22nd June. He is sending invitations to the squires who will be knighted at the ceremony and he has ordered Edward's coronation clothes.

I am looking forward to the ceremony. I will see Edward again, if only from a distance, and little Richard, too, perhaps. He is still in sanctuary with his mother and sisters, but they must surely come to see Edward crowned.

8th May 1483

Dear God, protect us now.

The wolves, as Annie called them, have hunted out Robert Stillington, an old, white-haired man who is now the Bishop of Bath. They brought him to a Council meeting this morning, and he admitted that he conducted a marriage ceremony between King Edward IV and Lady Eleanor Butler, daughter of John Talbot, 1st Earl of Shrewsbury, several months before Edward married Elizabeth Woodville.

The secret has burst open like a gaping wound.

My lovely boys will be stripped of all their rights. Neither Edward nor his brother will be crowned, ever.

This is the end.

19th May 1483

Edward has been moved to the Tower of London. Remembering what Annie told me about the death of King Henry in that place, I am filled with fear.

I sought out Dr Alcock, though I've always felt in awe of him, and confessed my worries. He was unexpectedly kind. He said the Archbishop of Canterbury had insisted on the move to ensure Edward's safety. His brother Richard is to join him in the Tower as soon as Elizabeth agrees.

'You need have no concern,' he went on. 'The boys will be safe there. And this may not be the end of the story, Lisa. There have been cases in the past when persons declared illegitimate have been re-legitimised by Act of Parliament. This could happen again. Young Edward may yet rule.'

'Really?'

It was a wonderful new hope. But my worry about the Tower had not gone.

'It's just – I mean – what if someone has the key?'

Dr Alcock looked affronted.

'What are you suggesting? I can assure you that the people entrusted with care of the boys are scrupulously honourable men. There can be no question of unauthorised access.'

I curtsied and said, 'Yes, sir. Of course.'

I learned later today that Uncle Richard has asked the City of York to send troops to protect him.

10ᵗʰ June 1483

I've found my way to Fleet Lane. My Uncle Bryn is little taller than Papa, a strong, brown-haired man, wearing a green baize apron.

He knows who I am at once, and enfolds me in a hug. 'Lisa! There's good to see you. I got your da's letter.'

Strangely, the Welsh lilt of his voice is stronger than my father's, despite years spent in London. His wife, Olwen, is Welsh as well. They have four children, about the same ages as my brothers and sisters. I stay to eat with them.

Bryn doesn't want to be called Uncle. He says, 'So Richard spread this scandal about Edward's marriage, did he? And he owned the cartloads of guns at Northampton?'

'No! You've got it all wrong.'

Bryn chuckles and Olwen scolds him. 'There's wicked you are.' She turns to me and adds, 'Don't mind him, *cariad*. He's only playing devil's advocate.'

'It's best you know what's being said,' Bryn says. 'Richard has a lot of enemies, and they are telling wild tales. But the King had faith in him. That's why he made him Protector to the boys.'

'Dr Alcock told me people born out of wedlock can be made legitimate again,' I tell them. 'A friend of mine says Henry Tudor's grandfather was. So Edward might still be crowned.'

'Go on? Well now, there's a thing.' Bryn thinks for a moment. Then he says, 'If that's true, your lovely lads are more of a danger to Henry than we thought.'

'Their mother will be pleased, though,' Olwen says, not seeing what Bryn means. 'She'll be so upset that young Edward won't be crowned.'

'Ah, but will she?' Bryn says. 'See, Edward is too young to rule on his own. That's why his da appointed Richard as his guardian. If Edward is crowned, Richard will advise Edward on all decisions. In effect, he will really be the king.'

'The power behind the throne,' Olwen says.

'Exactly. And that's the last thing Elizabeth wants. She'll get no favours out of Richard – she has no hold over him like she had over his brother.'

'So what will she do?' I ask.

'My guess is, she'll cosy up to the Lancasters and their Tudor boyo,' Bryn says. 'She won't mind if her sons are in the Tower. She can take them a toffee apple from time to time, and pat their heads.'

Olwen is shocked.

'There's terrible,' she says. 'Whatever kind of woman would be like that?

'The kind who is a ruthless politician,' says Bryn.

***

A few days after that, Richard is taken to join Edward in the Tower. The servants say his mother clung to him and protested, but only for a while. Then she let him go.

13th June 1483

Everyone is agog with talk.

This morning Uncle Richard, as I still think of him, burst into a room in the Tower with a body of armed men and confronted his enemies, who were closeted in a meeting. Lord Stanley and John Morton, the Bishop of Ely, were arrested, along with others. So was Lord Hastings, and that must have been terrible for Richard, for Hastings is – or was – one of his oldest friends.

Morton is telling everyone that Hastings was dragged down to the courtyard and beheaded at once on a chopping block, but this is a lie. The soldiers took him with the others, to stand trial next week. Richard has issued a proclamation giving details of the plot to assassinate him.

How did he know about it, I wonder? Somebody must have told him. Bryn thinks it was Stanley and Morton. That would explain why they were released at once. They were only arrested so nobody would suspect them. But what they did today may not be what they will do tomorrow.

There is something strange about Richard. He never seems to know who is trustworthy and who is not. For such a clever man, it is odd that he doesn't see what a glance or the flick of an eyebrow may mean. Maybe that is why he gets on so well with children, who are direct and don't use those unspoken messages. Or perhaps Warwick's betrayal when he was still no more than a boy left him constantly hoping that someone, somewhere, will be bound by loyalty, as his own motto proclaims.

'Poor Uncle Richard,' I say. 'Will nobody help him?

Olwen says, 'There's plenty would like to, *cariad*. But they don't dare.'

A different coronation

The reason Edward and Richard cannot inherit the throne has been explained clearly to the public. Notices have been put up everywhere, and a clergyman with the odd name of Ralph Shaa, whose half-brother is the Mayor of London, preached a sermon outside Old St Paul's Church, telling a great crowd of people about Edward IV's previous marriage.

The Parliament is drawing up a document detailing exactly why Richard must accept the throne. It is called *Titulus Regius*, which is Latin for *Royal Title*. Several copies of it are to be lodged in different places of safety so that even in the future, people can read it and know the truth.

Richard delayed for weeks about accepting the crown, but there was a public petition in favour of his coronation, and thousands of people signed. It was presented to him on the 26th of last month, and when he saw those countless pages of names, he at last gave in.

6th July 1483

Today was the coronation of Richard III of England.

I work as a chambermaid now and was busy making up beds and cleaning, so I saw nothing of it, but Bryn and Olwen said you could not get anywhere near the Abbey for the crowds. Richard obviously wanted to show he hoped for peace between York and Lancaster, because people from both families were invited. Margaret Beaufort, Henry Tudor's mother, carried the Queen's train, and that is a tremendous honour. But since she is now married to Lord Stanley, she may be laughing up her embroidered sleeve about Richard's hopes.

She has not had a very happy life, though. She was only twelve years old when Edmund Tudor took her as his wife, and he died a few months later, so she was alone when she gave birth to her baby son, and barely thirteen. The labour nearly killed her. She never had any more children, and people say it is because she was so badly injured.

***

The Duke of Buckingham, who arrested Rivers and the other Woodville traitors in Northampton, has betrayed Richard, as I feared. He and Stanley have been conspiring to overthrow the King – but, strangely, not on Henry Tudor's behalf. They are pushing for young Edward to be declared legitimate by Act of Parliament. I don't understand this. They must know that if Edward is crowned, Richard as his guardian will go on holding the power.

There may be a far more terrible explanation. For some time, nobody has seen the boys in the Tower playing outside in the courtyard on fine days as they used to, and it is rumoured that they may be dead. My mind runs in frantic circles. Is that why Buckingham and Stanley said they want them re-legitimised, to show people they are sure the boys are alive? Why would they bother to do this unless – I cannot bear to think of it – unless it is to disguise the fact that they know the boys are dead?

Elizabeth Woodville, still in sanctuary with her daughters, says nothing. Perhaps, being shut away from society, she knows nothing. I try to tell myself there is no need to be frightened by her silence. A worse thing worries me. After Buckingham's help at Northampton, Richard rewarded him with high office, and he appointed Stanley, who was on his side at the time, to the position of Constable of England.

As the Constable, Stanley is the official keeper of the Tower of London.

He holds the keys.

2ⁿᵈ November 1483

Buckingham's idea of re-legitimising the boys did not last long. He raised an army and went to support Henry Tudor, who had set out from France with a fleet of ships to invade England. God be thanked, there was a storm and Henry's armada had to turn back to the French coast. Buckingham had already landed in Wales and he went into hiding, but Richard offered a bounty for information on where he was. Somebody told, so Buckingham was arrested. Today he was beheaded for treason. I cannot be sorry.

Since then, Richard has issued a proclamation saying that anyone with a grievance will be heard and the matter dealt with. Its words are warming, declaring that the King is 'utterly determined all his true subjects shall live in rest and quiet and peaceably enjoy their lands, livelihoods and goods according to the laws of this his land.'

How can Richard's enemies hate such a reasonable man? Perhaps it is his virtue that annoys them. Two-faced John Morton, the Bishop of Ely, walks about with an air of saintliness, followed by his admiring little page, Thomas More, but I cannot think of him as a good man. He is writing a history of King Richard's life in Latin and young More, aged seven, boasts that he will translate it into English when he is older. I can imagine only too well what version of the truth it will contain.

***

Jane Shore is much talked about just now. She was one of King Edward's mistresses, and he adored her. She was at his deathbed. Elizabeth Woodville could not object, because Jane had carried messages from

70

her to Lord Hastings and to Elizabeth's son, Thomas Grey, both of whom were also Jane's lovers and fellow-conspirators. This came to light after Richard found Hastings closeted with his enemies. So she is another traitor.

Richard could have had Jane executed, but he was merciful. He made her do public penance by walking through London clad only in a thin shift, with a taper in her hand. But he misjudged how people would see it. They turned out by the hundred, as he rightly expected – but instead of deriding Jane, they cheered her on.

What did he expect? I went with some of the other servants to see her pass, and she looked saintly and aloof – and immensely alluring, as the thin fabric of her shift showed the form of her slim body very clearly. All the boys were whistling and shouting invitations.

Jane is in Ludgate prison now, but the lawyer sent by King Richard to judge the case has fallen madly in love with her and wants to marry her. Richard sent him a disapproving letter, but nobody imagines he will change his mind.

1ˢᵗ March 1484

Elizabeth Woodville came out of sanctuary today, after ten months of being shut away from the world. King Richard went to see her, and they spoke for a long time. They say he has given her a generous pension. Elizabeth and her daughters will live in Richard's court, though she made him swear that her girls will not be harmed. He gave her his assurance that they will be safe and well cared for.

I am glad she has accepted his help and friendship. Perhaps she has at last understood that he is more honest and generous than most of her own family, who have so greedily accepted every favour she could secure for them. She has written to her surviving son in France, too, asking him to come back and make his peace with Richard.

But there is so much we don't know. Has she gone to see her sons in the Tower? If she has, then she will know they are safe and still living, so why does she not make this public? Perhaps, after her months of seclusion, she is not aware of the rumours.

If she has not visited them, the questions are even more pressing. Why not? Has she been fobbed off?

Told that nobody can take her? The Queen Mother of England can hardly walk through the streets there alone. The most awful possibility is that she knows they are dead and keeps silent because their death makes it certain that they cannot be re-legitimised and spoil her plan to get into the favour of the Lancasters. No – surely even she would not go that far.

Why does not Richard make a public statement that he knows the boys to be alive? With his indifference to public opinion and his lack of perception about people's hidden fears and suspicions, he is playing into the hands of the Lancaster supporters. They, of course, are putting it about that Richard killed the boys because he wanted to be king.

I cannot believe such a thing. He has loved the boys throughout their lives, and was happy to be planning Edward's coronation – but I think he does not fit easily into the competitive hugger-mugger of London. Perhaps he belongs more naturally in the North, where people respect and admire him. Londoners think the North is savage and uncivilised, though, so this, too, goes against him.

9th April 1484

A tragedy. King Richard's son has died. It happened when Richard and Anne were away in the east of England on the royal 'progress' expected of a new king and queen. He is overwhelmed with grief, and Anne is white-faced, exhausted with weeping. She herself is not well, and seems hardly strong enough to bear such a blow. Always thin, there is nothing to her now but skin and bone, and she has a constant cough. The woman who does her laundry says the kerchiefs she presses to her lips are bloodstained. Anne's sister died of the same illness.

With this disaster added to my constant, cold fear about the boys, I long to be back in Ludlow with Tom. A letter from Papa yesterday spoke of trees coming into bud and seeds sown, lambs and a good heifer calf born. Tom never had any schooling so he cannot write and neither can Annie, but I think about them almost all the time, and find myself crying.

Bryn said, 'You need to go home, *cariad*.'

'But how? It's a long way, and I have no money.'

'There must be riders going down to Ludlow with messages. Wouldn't one of them take you?'

Olwen tutted. 'There's stupid you are, Bryn Jones. Those men ride fast and hard, same as they do everything else. She'd never be safe with them.'

'Ah,' said Bryn. 'I forgot about human nature. I need to think of something else, then.'

***

In the kitchen today, one of the maids said, 'Someone at the door for you.'

Oh, what magic! There stood Tom.

I couldn't believe it. With one gasp, I was in his arms.

'Your Uncle Bryn sent me some money,' he said. 'So I hired a horse. He's not fast, but he's big and strong. He'll take the two of us, no bother.'

We are at Bryn's tonight. I've brought my things, tied in a small bundle. We start out in the morning.

And, yes, Tom, yes – I will marry you.

***

On the broad back of the horse, my arms round Tom and my head leaning against his strong shoulder, my thoughts turn constantly to the boys. I feel disloyal, although in London I could do nothing for them and never even knew if they were alive. In that teeming city, I was as insignificant as a sparrow, or the breadcrumb it picks from the gutter.

Olwen tried to console me. She said, 'The princes were not free like ordinary children, *cariad*. They were little circus performers, waiting for the day when they'd be ringmaster.'

Perhaps she is right. But I look back to the early days and the fun Edward and I had, and the new pleasure when his little brother came to join us.

I loved them both, and I always will.

Homecoming, war and tragedy

Tom and I were married on May Day. My little sisters had flowers in their hair and the boys wore clean shirts, and everything looked beautiful. We'd baked and cooked for days and spread a great feast on trestle tables under the trees because we'd never have all got into the house. The birds sang. The sun shone.

In the months while I was away, Tom built a cottage. It's nearly done. He is thatching its roof now. He still works at the Castle, and I am back there as a kitchen hand.

Annie looked up from beating eggs when I came into the kitchen and said, 'Lisa!' She gave me a great hug – then of course she wanted to know the latest news from London.

'When will Henry Tudor's wedding be? Any time soon?'

'Christmas Day.'

'Huh. Trust him to make a big splash. I hate that man.' Then her face turned serious. 'But what's this about the princes, Lisa? People are saying Richard murdered them. You and I know he'd never do that – he adored them. They're trying to make him out a monster.'

'Yes, they are. Annie – I'm so worried.'

'We can only pray for them.'

She was right. A constant prayer was in my mind and it still repeats itself again and again.

Dear Lord, if it be Thy Will, watch over my lovely boys and keep them safe. Amen. Dear Lord...

Dear Lord...

19ᵗʰ March 1485

King Richard's wife died three days ago. The malicious gossip gets worse and worse. They are saying Richard poisoned Anne so that he can marry

Elizabeth Woodville's daughter, to prevent her from marrying Henry Tudor.

This final unkindness broke Richard's reserve. He was so furious that he called the mayor and aldermen of London to the Great Hall of the Mercers' Company, and berated them for their cruel slander. Their records preserve the occasion, and the wording has been circulated among his supporters. Bryn sent them to me in a letter. Richard said it 'never came into his thought or mind to marry in such a manner'. He had adored Anne ever since they were children, and to have it said that he killed her added an unbearable anguish.

He is now utterly alone. I wish I had some way to tell him that I trust him and believe in him. But I am nobody, and in the life of kings, everyone has to be somebody. King Edward broke that rule when he married Elizabeth Woodville, and we have paid for it to this day.

There is still silence about the boys. Surely, if they had been killed, rumours would have spread? The people who work at the Tower will have the same detailed knowledge of the place as we have of Ludlow. How could two bodies be smuggled out without their knowing? How could their cell be empty one morning without questions being asked? I still persuade myself that they are alive.

Meanwhile, Henry Tudor has been gathering an army over there in France, preparing to cross the Channel again and invade England. There is going to be a war. I feel that all human kindness has gone. I fear for the future and for ourselves as well as for the helpless boys caught up in wicked schemes.

Papa tells me not to distress myself, for I will have a baby of my own in the autumn, and the child growing inside me must not be disturbed by fretting and worry. But the prayer goes on in my mind.

Dear Lord, if it be Thy Will...

7th August 1485

Henry has landed an army of three thousand men on the west coast of Wales, near Milford. It would have been quicker to cross the Channel to southern England, but Tom says three thousand men are not enough for a major battle. Henry aims to gather Welsh supporters as he marches through the country, because he himself is Welsh. The servants at the castle laugh at this, because as far as they are concerned,

Henry is from France. He speaks English, it seems, but nobody has heard him say a word of Welsh. Quite a few have joined his army, all the same.

King Richard was in the North when news of the invasion came. He has done wonderfully well there, settling the age-old quarrel with the marauding Scots and getting the border town of Berwick returned to England. His Council of the North is much respected. But he will have to gather an army together as fast as he can now and start on the long march south-westward, to meet his enemy.

16th August 1485

Henry and his troops have crossed the border into England. King Richard's army is still on the road, making its way towards a town called Leicester. Soldiers from Northumberland and York are on the march as well, coming to join him. Stanley has formed a force of his own. He says he supports Richard, though everyone knows that he will go with whichever side he thinks will win.

Annie said, 'I hear Henry is no fighter. He skulks round the edge, they say, trying not to get his shoes dirty. That's why Stanley is on Richard's side. If anything goes wrong, though, he'll turn like a flipped coin.'

There is something awful about this slow moving of thousands of men from the west of Wales and from all over England, to a chosen place where they will meet other men then hack and slash at each other until one side is beaten. I try not to think about it. I stay at home now, in the little house Tom built, because my baby is due very soon. I clean and cook and tend the garden, and try to imagine the war is not happening.

24th August 1485

Annie is at our door, in tears.

'He is dead, Lisa. They savaged him. Richard. Our King Richard. Oh, dear God.'

We are in each other's arms. The baby inside me moves uneasily as if it shares my distress.

After a while Annie gently detaches herself. She mops her eyes and we sit down at the table.

'A man came to the castle yesterday. He'd been at the battle. Still filthy. Richard was betrayed, Lisa.'

'Stanley.'

'Yes. Richard saw Henry watching while soldiers hacked and battered at each other. Perhaps he thought if he could kill him, it would bring the war to an end. He charged towards Henry with some good men but the mud was so deep, the horses were floundering and couldn't get on. Richard dismounted and went for Henry on foot. He killed his standard-bearer and another man. Then Stanley saw he was alone and yelled for his men to attack him. Richard fought like a demon, the man who came said. But they were all round him, Lisa. He didn't have a chance.'

Annie takes a shuddering breath.

'And the worst thing,' she goes on. 'When he was dead, they stripped him naked and slung him across a horse like a stag killed in a hunt. They took him into Leicester like that, for onlookers to see and hack at with their own swords, shouting and cheering. They dumped him in a church. We don't even know – '

Her voice breaks and ends on a sob.

' – where he is to be buried.'

Afterwards

As I said at the start, it was a long time ago.

Mama died the year after the Bosworth battle, but Papa still helps the people who need him.

Annie left the castle, saying she would have nothing to do with 'that murderer' or his court. She had no job to go to, but Jane Shore came back to Ludlow with her adoring lawyer husband, and they took her on as a cook. Annie is shocked by Jane, though somehow she likes her.

'What she got up to,' she says. 'Unbelievable. But we do have a laugh.'

My two sweet daughters are almost young women now, and Huw, their younger brother, is as tall as Tom. He says he will keep the pages I have written and show them to children of his own one day. I tell him not to take anything for granted, but I like thinking of it.

I know more now about what happened at Bosworth. On the night before the battle, Stanley told everyone he was ill in bed with the sweating sickness and would not be able to fight – but he was not ill at all. He was with Henry, planning battle tactics. Afterwards, when Richard had been killed and the fighting had ended, a soldier saw something glinting in a bush. It was the gold circlet Richard had worn over his helmet. Stanley snatched it from him and gave it to Henry, who crammed it over his own helmet and crowed that he was now King Henry the Seventh.

He tried to confiscate all the property of Richard and the men who had fought for him, claiming that they were guilty of treason against himself as the ruling monarch. But Richard was the ruling monarch until the moment of his death, so any treason before that could only be against him, not Henry. Truth had ceased to matter, though. The confiscation request Henry put to Parliament gave the date of his kingship as the day *before* the Bosworth battle. A sharp-eyed clerk changed it to the correct one, thank goodness.

The next thing was, Henry repealed Bishop Stillington's confession that he had officiated at King Edward's previous marriage. He declared the *Titulus Regius* an illegal document and forbade anyone to read it and burned every copy he could find.

Papa was perplexed.

'He must think the *Titulus Regius* simply set out Richard's right to be king,' he said. 'Perhaps he does not read Latin. But it was also Parliament's testimony that young Edward and Richard were illegitimate. In destroying that document, Henry has made it possible for Edward's sons to inherit the throne. So their supporters may challenge Henry's right to be king. Your lovely boys could yet be recognised as royal.'

For one brief moment, the heavy certainty that they are dead lifted and I had a thrill of excitement – but Papa was frowning.

'If Henry sees his mistake, or someone points it out – which they will do – he will have to get rid of the boys. He may already have done it.'

That nightmare moment is still with me. We will never know the truth, because Henry and his helpers have constructed an alternative version, in which King Edward's first marriage never happened. There was no secret that gave Elizabeth Woodville such power over the King, they say. Clarence and Warwick only rebelled in order to defend the country against Richard's evil determination to rule. There is one mystery, though.

Henry issued a long list of Richard's 'wrongs, odious offences and abominations against God and men and in special our said sovereign lord.' (Henry himself.) And yet, the detailed list made no mention that Richard might have killed the princes, although suspicion was running wild about what had happened to them. Henry's trump card would have been to say Richard was their murderer. But he did not do it. Much later, his supporters painted Richard as the killer of his nephews, but not at the time. Why was that? Was Henry aware of a different truth, and avoided any mention of the boys for fear of starting a troublesome enquiry? We will never know.

The fate of Elizabeth Woodville is also strange. Despite her energetic efforts to support Henry Tudor, he confiscated all her lands and property and made them over to her daughter, whom he had married. Then he banished her to an abbey in Bermondsey for the rest of her life. What had Elizabeth done to cause such drastic retribution? The reason Henry gave seemed feeble for a man well used to shifts of allegiance for diplomatic purposes – it never worried him that Stanley veered from one side to the other as it suited him. All he could say against Elizabeth was that she and her daughters had lived for some months in Richard's palace when they came out of sanctuary and were thus 'contaminated' by him.

There is another possibility. Elizabeth must at some point have found out the terrible truth about her boys. Either she knew all along, and colluded in it for the sake of keeping in with the Tudors – which seems impossible for any mother – or someone whispered that Henry was responsible for their deaths.

If that happened, it would have been typical of her to confront him in righteous fury. She would then have been as dangerous to Henry as poor Clarence had been to her, years earlier. He had to silence her, before she could spread her dangerous knowledge. Elizabeth would have gambled on the assumption that he could not kill her, for it would have raised too much of a scandal, but perhaps she never thought he might banish her from public life. Too late, she saw her danger and protested desperately that Richard had dragged her to his court by force – but Henry was in a class of his own when it came to inventive lying. Elizabeth vanished behind the closed walls of Bermondsey Abbey and spoke no further word to anyone in the outside world. Her death a few years later was hardly noticed.

Others have been lavishly rewarded. Dr Alcock is Controller of the Royal Works and Buildings. Morton is the Archbishop of Canterbury and also the Lord Chancellor. People loathe him for the double-edged tax system known as 'Morton's Fork', which holds that a man who lives frugally will be saving money, so he must pay as much tax as the wealthiest. Henry is paying several writers as well as Morton to produce approved versions of Richard's life. One of them, Polydore Vergil, is Italian, and knows only what he is told.

More grubby little events have occurred. A man called James Tyrrell was executed for the murder of my lovely boys, years afterwards, but Henry had been hunting down all York supporters, and Tyrrell had served King Richard loyally throughout his life.

89

When he supported Edmund de la Pole, third Duke of Suffolk, as the leading Yorkist claimant to the throne, Henry arrested him and charged him with killing the princes. Tyrrell swore that he had nothing to do with it, but hours of torture in the Tower forced him to sign a confession.

Twice, boys have turned up whose supporters claim they are one of the lost princes, smuggled to safety. I did not see either of them, of course. I would have known in a flash if they were Edward or Richard, even after all these years. The first one, Lambert Simnel, was so young that they simply condemned him to work as a scullion in the castle kitchen. The other, Perkin Warbeck, was beheaded.

In all this, I am certain of only one thing. King Richard the Third, slight of stature though he was, stood head and shoulders above the rest of them. People in the north knew that. Bryn sent me a copy of the address that Archibald Whitelaw gave when welcoming Richard to York on 12th September 1484, the year before Bosworth. He spoke of 'your innate benevolence, your clemency, your liberality, your good faith, your supreme justice and your incredible greatness of heart'.

I keep that piece of paper tucked away in secret, together with another that I stole when copies were being smuggled round Ludlow. That one has words by Thomas Langton, Bishop of St David's. Richard, he said, 'contents the people wherever he goes better than ever did any prince… God has sent him to us for the welfare of us all.'

We have not been noted for our kindness to those whom God sends.

The cutting short of King Richard's life leaves us diminished, but those of us who loved him are still warmed when we think of him, and we rage helplessly against the power-seeking that destroys good men and lovely boys. My children say people not yet born may have more sense, and learn to understand.

I hope they are right.

Historical Note

In this book, Lisa and her family are invented characters, as are the court servants. Throughout history, 'common people' have watched and heard and understood what was going on, but they leave no trail of evidence behind them and their names are unknown. Carefully re-inventing them is the only way we can go back into an earlier time. All the events concerning the named, real people are true, though any writer today must sift the evidence very carefully. It is always possible that a contemporary account may have been written to the order of some powerful person, the facts selected or ignored for political purposes.

The riddle of the princes in the Tower has always posed this problem. Ever since the boys disappeared in 1483, people have taken sides over the question of whether Richard III murdered his two young nephews. Those who believe he did – and there are many – can point to good company. Shakespeare showed Richard as an evil schemer, twisted in mind as well as body, and this image has persisted. The belief that he killed his nephews so that he himself would rule England has a simple, persuasive logic. Perceiving the fallacies that surround it demands a little more thought.

Henry VII killed Richard at the battle of Bosworth Field in 1485. Once on the throne, Henry began a systematic wiping-out of the Plantagenet family to which Richard had belonged. His son, Henry VIII, continued it. In 1541, fifty-six years after Bosworth, he ordered the beheading of Margaret Pole, a quiet lady now nearly 70 years old who had committed no crime except for being the daughter of King Richard's brother George, Duke of Clarence. Shakespeare was not born until 1564, but the persecution of any potential supporter of the Plantagenet line would have been common knowledge. He depicted 'Richard Crookback' as a deformed villain, because he could not do otherwise.

The Tudor line came to an end with Elizabeth's death in 1603 and for the first time, dissenters dared to raise their voices. In 1619 George Buck wrote a book in Richard's support, and fresh thinking began to grow. Horace Walpole defended Richard's reputation in 1768, and in the twentieth century an increasing number of writers questioned the orthodox belief in his guilt. Many people, however, continue to believe the Tudor version.

As soon as Henry VII became king, he destroyed every copy of the *Titulus Regius* that he could find. That document was drawn up by Parliament (not by Richard as sometimes alleged), and constitutes official proof of Edward's previous marriage. One copy survived, so we know its contents. It states that Richard was forced to accept the throne, because his nephews had been declared illegitimate. Henry imposed severe penalties even for speaking of the document, and succeeded in pushing the dark old secret back into its box.

He had two good reasons for this. *Titulus Regius* not only proved Richard's claim to the throne, but meant that the young princes' sisters were also illegitimate – and the eldest of them was Henry's own wife, a marriage eagerly sought by her mother, Elizabeth Woodville.

Almost every history written since that time has glossed over the fact that Edward IV was already married when he took Elizabeth Woodville as his wife. It has been dismissed as dubious hearsay, although the priest who conducted the marriage admitted in court that he had officiated at the private ceremony. After Richard's death, the Tudor spin-machine was assiduous in presenting its own version of the facts. Strangely, it did not at first allege that Richard had killed his nephews, though it would have been an ace card to play, blackening his reputation forever, as it did eventually. It must be asked why they overlooked this opportunity. There can be only two reasons – either the princes were still alive at that time, or the Tudors knew who had killed them and had not yet thought of blaming Richard.

Sir Thomas More's biography of Richard III was highly critical, and has been the basis for most of the later assumptions. But More, born in 1478, was only five years old when Richard was crowned. He could not have been an eyewitness to the scenes he described. These come from accounts written by

More's master, John Morton, whom Henry appointed Archbishop of Canterbury in gratitude for his many services. Other chroniclers are equally dubious, as all of them were carrying out paid commissions for King Henry.

The whole case against Richard rests on the truth or untruth of the Tudor version of events. Henry VII's suppression of the *Titulus Regius* and of the secret that it exposed shows a desperate need to establish a different picture. Henry appointed chroniclers who were paid to write history as they were told to. Elizabeth Woodville was locked away in a convent for the rest of her life and could speak to nobody. The secret that had dominated Richard's entire life was thrust back in its box, where it has remained. With the X-ray vision of the 21st century, we should now be able to see through the closed lid.